POLICE Officers ON · Patrol

by **Kersten Hamilton** ★ pictures by **R. W. Alley**

Viking

Viking

Published by Penguin Group

Penguin Young Readers Group, 345 Hudson Street, New York, New York 10014, U.S.A.

Penguin Group (Canada), 90 Eglinton Avenue East, Suite 700, Toronto, Ontario, Canada M4P 2Y3 (a division of Pearson Penguin Canada Inc.)

Penguin Books Ltd, 80 Strand, London WC2R 0RL, England

Penguin Ireland, 25 St Stephen's Green, Dublin 2, Ireland (a division of Penguin Books Ltd)

Penguin Group (Australia), 250 Camberwell Road, Camberwell, Victoria 3124, Australia (a division of Pearson Australia Group Pty Ltd)

Penguin Books India Pvt Ltd, 11 Community Centre, Panchsheel Park, New Delhi – 110 017, India

Penguin Group (NZ), 67 Apollo Drive, Rosedale, North Shore 0632, New Zealand (a division of Pearson New Zealand Ltd)

Penguin Books (South Africa) (Pty) Ltd, 24 Sturdee Avenue, Rosebank, Johannesburg 2196, South Africa

Penguin Books Ltd, Registered Offices: 80 Strand, London WC2R 0RL, England

First published in 2009 by Viking, a division of Penguin Young Readers Group

13

LIBRARY OF CONGRESS CATALOGING-IN-PUBLICATION DATA
Hamilton, K. R. (Kersten R.)
Police officers on patrol / by Kersten Hamilton ; illustrated by R.W. Alley.
p. cm.
Summary: Illustrations and brief rhyming text depict police officers
responding to a variety of situations, from a broken traffic light to a robbery.
ISBN 978-0-670-06315-4 (hardcover)
[1. Stories in rhyme. 2. Police—Fiction.]
I. Alley, R. W. (Robert W.), ill. II. Title.
PZ8.3.H1853Po 2009
[E]—dc22
2008023240

Set in Godlike
Manufactured in China
Book design by Nancy Brennan

For Tobias: rock and roll, Bubby!—K.H.

Uniform!

Badge!

Radio!

Police officers,
getting ready to go!

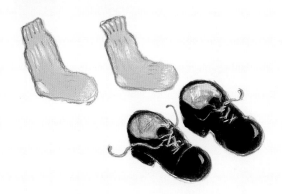

Squad report—
Sergeant Santole.
"People need help!
Let's rock and roll!"

A broken light might
cause a crash!
Who can help?
Who is fast?

Officer Mike,
on traffic patrol!

Uniform!

Badge!

Radio!

Officer responding!

Go, Mike, go!

Situation?
Under control!
"When people need help,
we rock and roll!"

This little boy can't
find his mom!
He needs help!
Who will come?

Officer Jan
on mounted patrol!

Uniform!

Badge!

Radio!

Officer responding!

Go, Jan, go!

Situation?

Under control!

"When people need help,
we rock and roll!"

Robbers robbing on
Mulgrave!
Who will help?
Who is brave?

Officer Carl
on crime patrol!

Situation?
Under control!

"When people need help,
we rock and roll!"

Uniform!
Badge!
Radio!
"If YOU need help,
we're on patrol!"